Motherbridge
of Love

Text provided by The Mothers' Bridge of Love

Illustrated by Josée Masse

Barefoot Books
step inside a story

Once there were two women
who never knew each other.

Motherbridge
of Love

To all the children we love — M. B. L.
For Sophie and Sergeï, without whom the family would be incomplete! — J. M.

Barefoot Books
294 Banbury Road
Oxford, OX2 7ED

Barefoot Books
2067 Massachusetts Ave
Cambridge, MA 02140

First published in Great Britain by Barefoot Books, Ltd
and in the United States of America by Barefoot Books, Inc in 2007
The paperback edition first published 2013

Graphic design by Barefoot Books, Bath
Reproduction by B & P International, Hong Kong
Printed in China on 100% acid-free paper
This book was typeset in Albertina MT Regular and Present
The illustrations were prepared in acrylics on Strathmore paper

Hardback ISBN 978-1-84686-047-8
Paperback ISBN 978-1-78285-040-3

British Cataloguing-in-Publication Data:
a catalogue record for this book is available from the British Library

Library of Congress Cataloging-in-Publication Data is available under
LCCN 2006038846

1 3 5 7 9 8 6 4 2

One you do not know.
The other you call Mother.

Two different lives shaped to make you one.

One became your guiding star;
the other became your sun.

The first one gave you life;
the second taught you to live it.

The first gave you a need for love;
the second was there to give it.

One gave you a body, the other taught you games.

One gave you a talent. The other taught you aims.

One gave you emotions;
the other calmed your fears.

One saw your first sweet smile;

the other dried your tears.

One found a home for you
that she could not provide.

The other prayed for a child;

her hope was not denied.

And now you ask, of course you do,
The question others ask me too:

This place or your birth place –
which are you a daughter of?

Both of them, my darling –

and two different kinds of love.

Source Note

The poem you have just read was submitted anonymously by an adoptive mother to the charity The Mothers' Bridge of Love (MBL). The text at the front of the book presents the poem in simplified Chinese. Founded in 2004, MBL is a charity that reaches out to Chinese children all over the world, in order to develop a connection between China and the West, and between adoptive culture and birth culture. It has three missions: to promote cultural awareness and understanding between the East and the West; to bridge the gap between adoptive parents and the adopted Chinese children, helping the children find their cultural roots; and to provide educational and other forms of support to children living in poor rural areas of China.

Among its many objectives, MBL coordinates a travel initiative, which allows Chinese children who have grown up abroad to become more familiar with the real China — the countryside, where most of the adopted children were born. This initiative also gives adoptive parents a chance to learn more about their children's heritage.

To learn more about
The Mothers' Bridge of Love and its many
offerings, you can visit their website at:
www.mothersbridge.org